The Night Out

Written by Jack Gabolinscy

Illustrated by Fraser Williamson

Mom was going away for the weekend. Dad and I and my brother Tony were going to be

HOME ALONE.

"Be good!" said Mom.

She shook her finger at Dad. "The last time I went away you painted the bathroom purple with big orange bubbles. It was horrible!"

"Our bathroom is cool," said Dad. "I don't know why you don't like it."

2

When Mom had gone, Dad sat down in his favorite chair. He picked up the newspaper. "Let's go to the movies after dinner," he said.

We looked in Dad's newspaper and found a horror movie:

Con the Swamp Monster.

"Looks like fun!" said Dad. "Let's go!"

Get out of my face!

After dinner, we all had showers. When Dad came out of the bedroom, he was wearing yucky yellow pants, a bright red shirt, and an old jacket. He had pink sneakers on his feet with holes in the toes and green laces.

"You look like a scarecrow in those clothes," I said.

I was not going anywhere with him looking like that!

"What's wrong with my clothes?" asked Dad. "I like comfort. I don't dress to look pretty."

Dad went to change.
He came back with a pair
of white sneakers and a green
jacket. The jacket came down
to his knees.

"How is this?" he asked.

My brother Tony
laughed.

"It's not that bad!"
said Dad.

Dad went to change again.
He put the old jacket back
on. It was still awful!

But it was not as bad
as the long green jacket.
He had looked like a long
green caterpillar.

It's not funny....

8

9

When we got to the movies, we saw a lot of people. They were all dressed up. The women had on long dresses and lots of jewelry. The men had on sharp suits. They had hankies sticking out of their jacket pockets.

Tony and I stood at the door. We pretended Dad wasn't with us. People were staring at him.

"I didn't think a movie like Con the Swamp Monster would be so popular," said Dad.

We got our tickets and we had to sit right up in the front row. We had to bend our necks back to look up at the screen.

The first movie was about tea making. It was boring. I tried to open my bag of popcorn.

"Ssshhh!" somebody said.

I tried to be quiet, but . . .

"Ssshhh!" growled somebody again.

" Ssshhh ! "

rustle

rustle

13

"Give me the bag!" said Dad. He crunched and scrunched the bag in his hands.

"Ssshhh! Be quiet!" said the angry voices.

Then Dad opened Tony's bag! The usher came down the steps. She shined her flashlight on us. "Ssshhh!" she said.

"Would you like some popcorn, Miss?" asked Dad in a loud voice.

We were **embarrassed**. We thought we were going to be kicked out.

rustle

ustle

M

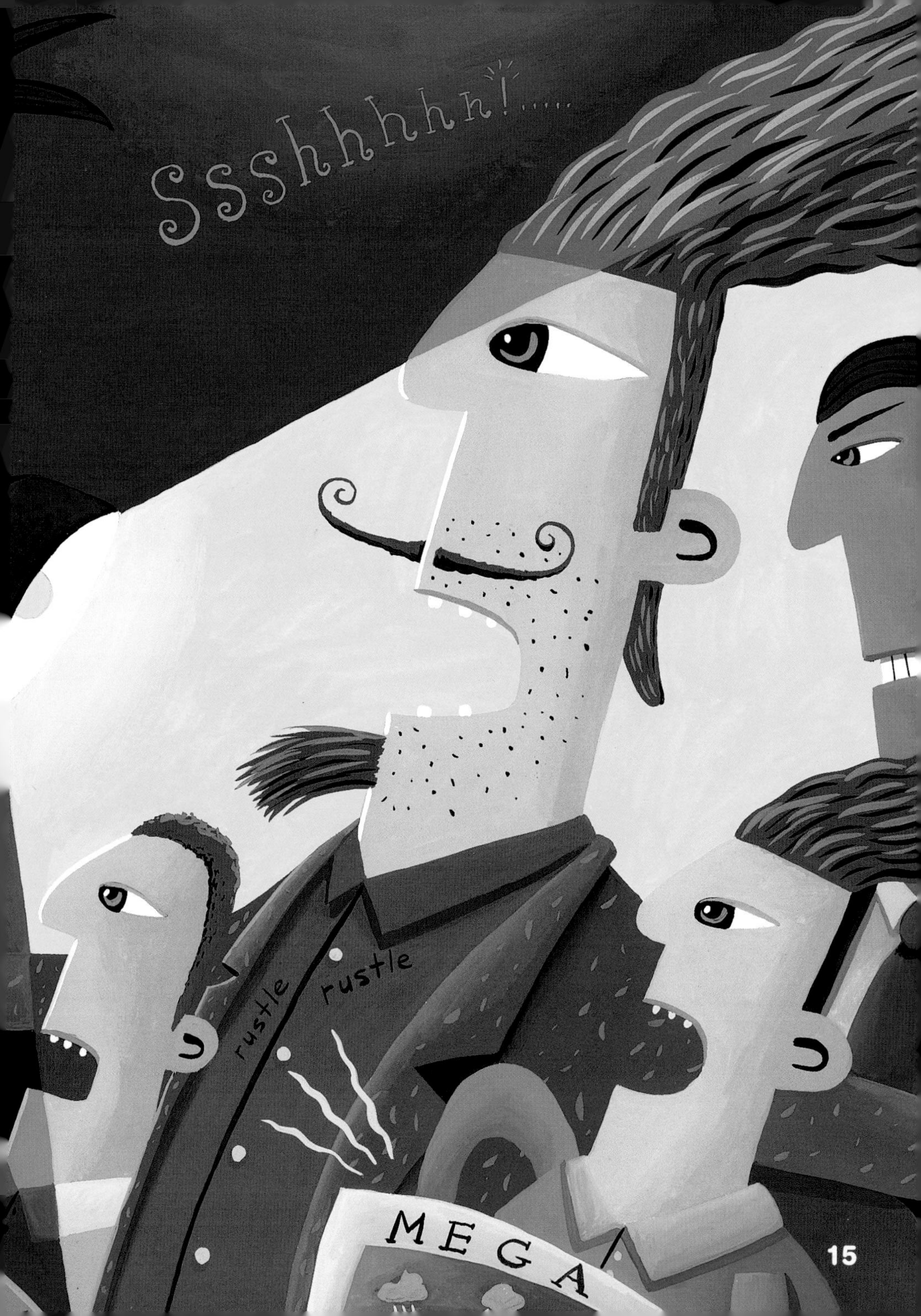
Ssshhhhh!.....
rustle
rustle
MEGA

When the movie started, it wasn't *Con the Swamp Monster*. It was an opera. The people had great voices and sang beautiful songs. But Dad said he didn't understand opera, so we went home and watched TV. At home, no one growled about popcorn. And Dad couldn't embarrass us anymore.

I looked in the newspaper to see why the Swamp Monster movie was not on. It had been on all right – three weeks ago. Dad's newspaper was three weeks old.

WHAT A NIGHT OUT!

Great shot!

Recounts

Recounts tell about something that has happened.

A recount tells the reader

- what happened

- to whom

- where it happened

- when it happened

A recount has events in sequence . . .

. . . and a conclusion

Guide Notes

Title: The Night Out
Stage: Fluency (1)

Text Form: Recount
Approach: Guided Reading
Processes: Thinking Critically, Exploring Language, Processing Information
Written and Visual Focus: Recount Structure, Text Highlights, Illustrative Text,
  Speech Bubbles

THINKING CRITICALLY
(sample questions)
- Why do you think the boys didn't want to go out with Dad?
- How do you think Tony felt about his Dad's clothes? How do you know how he felt?
- Why do you think they had to sit in the front row at the movies?
- Why do you think Dad didn't understand opera?
- What do you think the kids will do next time Dad suggests a night out?

EXPLORING LANGUAGE

Terminology
Spread, author and illustrator credits, ISBN number

Vocabulary
Clarify: embarrass, opera, horror, scrunched, comfort
Nouns: bathroom, movies, chair, newspaper
Verbs: pick, sit, open, growl, crunch, scrunch, sing
Singular/plural: bubble/bubbles, movie/movies, person/people
Simile: looked like a long green caterpillar, look like a scarecrow
Abbreviation: TV (television)

Print Conventions
Apostrophes – possessives (Dad's newspaper, Tony's bag), contractions (don't, didn't)
Colon